Eyes Like Mine

AND

Also by Kay Bratt

Mei Li and the Wise Laoshi

Silent Tears: A Journey of Hope in a Chinese Orphanage

Chasing China: A Daughter's Quest for Truth

The Bridge

A Thread Unbroken

Train to Nowhere

Tales of the Scavenger's Daughters

Willow Series

Eyes Like Mine

Story by Kay Bratt

Illustrated by Tanya Gleadall

AND

Printed in the United States of America
First Printing, 2013

ISBN 978-1490372174

www.KayBratt.com

Book design and layout by Odyssey Books (www.odysseybooks.com.au)

Dedicated to the many little boys I knew and loved in China.

You have never left my thoughts or my heart.

I looked at our family picture,

And what did I find?

My face is very different

And I don't see eyes like mine.

Mama's hair is curly,

And Daddy's is dark brown.

Brother's face is heart-shaped,

But mine is really round.

Their skin is white like dumplings,

And they stand so very tall,

I don't think I fit in,

Because I am very small.

I climbed up in my tree house,

And was never coming down!

But daddy came to look for me,

And quickly I was found.

He told me my birth story,
Of when I lived in another land.
How when he found out I was waiting,
He came to take my hand.

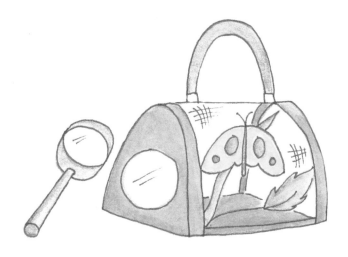

"Son, your mom and I saw you in a picture,
And the love grew big in our hearts.
We got in a plane and flew a very long way,
So we'd never again be apart.

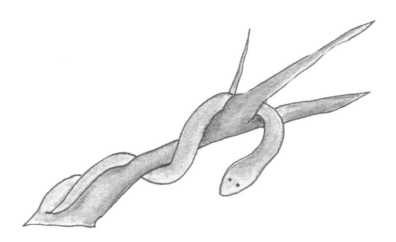

We love everything about you,

Your hair, your eyes and your nose.

Everything on you is perfect,

Right on down to your tiny toes!"

I took another look at the photo,

And this time what did I see?

It doesn't matter what we look like,

Because I know my Daddy loves me!

About the Author

Kay Bratt is a child advocate and author, living in an ivy-covered cottage by the lake in South Carolina, in the big 'ole United States of America. When she isn't writing stories, she's chasing her rowdy dog Riley as he hunts her sneaky cat Gypsy through the trees and around the lake. To see more of her work, join her on Facebook or go to her website at www.kaybratt.com

About the Illustrator

Tanya Gleadall is an artist and illustrator, living near the foothills of Canada's Rocky Mountains. When she isn't drawing she can be found refereeing food fights between her two cats or making delicious fruit smoothies for her husband and two very amusing children.
You can see more of her work at www.tanyagleadall.com

CPSIA information can be obtained
at www.ICGtesting.com
Printed in the USA
LVHW070425260419
615629LV00021BA/587/P